COWBOY CAR

E Ransom 2017

by Jeanie Franz Ransom

illustrated by Ovi Nedelcu

two lions

Published by Two Lions, New York

www.apub.com

Amazon, the Amazon logo, and Two Lions are trademarks of Amazon.com, Inc., or its affiliates.

ISBN-13: 9781503950979 (hardcover)
ISBN-10: 1503950972K (hardcover)

The illustrations are rendered in mixed media.

Book design by Jen Keenan

Printed in China
First Edition
1 3 5 7 9 10 8 6 4 2

For my posse: Bob, Matt, Brian, and Alex
—J.F.R.

To all the little cowboys and cowgirls
that like to dream big
—O.N.

Ever since he was knee-high to his daddy's hubcaps, Little Car wanted to be a **COWBOY**.

Growing up in a crowded city garage, Little Car had seen cowboys on TV. He loved their big, wide hats and pointy-toed boots.

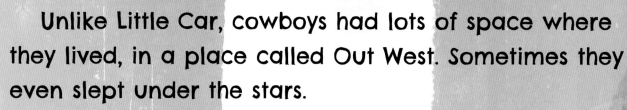

Unlike Little Car, cowboys had lots of space where they lived, in a place called Out West. Sometimes they even slept under the stars.

When Little Car went outside, it was noisy and busy. Sometimes he couldn't even hear his own horn!

"CARS CAN'T BE COWBOYS,"

everyone told Little Car.

Little Car's dad wanted him to follow in his tracks and be a taxicab in the city.

His mom wanted him to be a family car and settle down in a garage close to home.

But Little Car couldn't stop dreaming about driving the range with other cowboys, herding cattle by day, and circling up around the campfire at night.

So when Little Car got a lot bigger,
he decided to pack his trunk and
head Out West.

"Don't forget to stop at red lights!"
honked Dad.
"Keep your doors locked!" Mom called
as her windshield wipers sped up
to catch her tears.

The first thing Little Car did Out West was look for a real cowboy hat.

"Howdy," Little Car said in his best cowboy voice. "I need a hat, please."

"I think you're going to need a *fifty*-gallon hat," the man said. "I don't have one that big."

"How about that one?" Little Car asked.

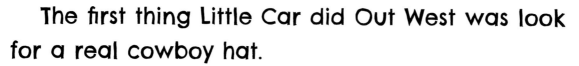

"I reckon I can sell it to you," the man said.
"Thank you kindly," Little Car said.

Little Car drove until he found a ranch. There were cowboys everywhere, all wearing hats just like his!

"My name's Dusty," said a cowboy. "What can I do for you, buckaroo?"

"I'm here to be a cowboy!"

"CARS CAN'T BE COWBOYS.

THEY CAN'T RIDE HORSES!" Dusty said.

Little Car's bumpers drooped. It was true. He *couldn't* ride a horse.

"It's a shame, too," Dusty said. "We could use an extra hand."

Little Car's gears clicked. "Let me prove I can do it."

"I'll give you a try," Dusty said. "Come back tomorrow."

The next morning, Little Car watched cowboys twirl ropes in the air, race around barrels, and try to ride something called a "mechanical bull."

"YEE-HAW! YIPPY-YI-YAY!

GET ALONG, LI'L DOGGIES!" Little Car shouted.

The cowboys laughed.

"Come on," Dusty said. "It's time to see what you can do!"

"Let's see how quick you are," Dusty said.

Little Car zoomed around the barrels in no time. He was used to making quick turns around tight corners in the city.

"Not bad," Dusty said.

The next day, Dusty gave Little Car some cowboy chores. "Let's see how strong you are," he said.

Little Car had plenty of power in his engine.

Maybe a little too much power. . . .

Later, Dusty took Little Car out on the range.
"Let's see how fast you can round up those
li'l doggies. Better hurry! It's getting dark!"
Little Car wasn't worried about the dark.

HE HAD HEADLIGHTS!

"You did a pretty good job this week," Dusty said that night. "Let's see how you do tomorrow at the rodeo."

Little Car did a brake dance.
Was he finally going to be a

COWBOY?

The next morning, Little Car helped
carry a few things to the rodeo.

But the man told Little Car, "You can't be in the rodeo unless you ride a horse."

"Aw, shucks! I'm sorry," Dusty said. "I hope you'll stay to watch me ride Double Trouble. He's the biggest, meanest bull you've ever seen!"

So Little Car stayed. The bull that came out
bucking and kicking didn't look *anything* like
the one back at the ranch. This bull was *real*!

Dusty went up, and came down with a big

THUD.

The rodeo clown couldn't get to him.
Double Trouble turned and headed straight
toward Dusty.
Oh no! Little Car thought.
Dusty needs help!

VROOOMMM!

With tires squealing, horn honking, and the radio blasting, Little Car got everyone's attention—including the bull's.

Little Car turned left, right, then swerved, stopped, backed up, and drove around and around until the bull's snorts turned into snores.

HE SAVED DUSTY!

After the rodeo, everyone wanted to talk to Little Car.
"So, is it true that you're a cowboy at the
Circle R Ranch?" a reporter asked.
Before Little Car could answer, Dusty came over.

"He sure is," Dusty said. "In fact, he's my pardner!"
Little Car grinned from gear to gear. He really
could be a COWBOY!

That afternoon, a video of Little Car went viral on MooTube. Back at the garage, Little Car's parents were surprised to see their son on TV. "That's our boy!" Mom said.

"THAT'S OUR *COWBOY!*" Dad said.

And Little Car drove off into the sunset,
home on the range at last.